W9-AXY-688

Mama's Little Duckling

Marjorie Blain Parker ❖ ILLUSTRATIONS BY Mike Wohnoutka

Dutton Children's Books

DUTTON CHILDREN'S BOOKS
A division of Penguin Young Readers Group

Published by the Penguin Group
Penguin Group (USA) Inc., 375 Hudson Street, New York, New York 10014, U.S.A.
Penguin Group (Canada), 90 Eglinton Avenue East, Suite 700, Toronto, Ontario, Canada M4P 2Y3 (a division of Pearson Penguin Canada Inc.)
Penguin Books Ltd, 80 Strand, London WC2R 0RL, England • Penguin Ireland, 25 St Stephen's Green, Dublin 2, Ireland (a division of Penguin Books Ltd)
Penguin Group (Australia), 250 Camberwell Road, Camberwell, Victoria 3124, Australia (a division of Pearson Australia Group Pty Ltd) • Penguin Books India
Pvt Ltd, 11 Community Centre, Panchsheel Park, New Delhi - 110 017, India • Penguin Group (NZ), 67 Apollo Drive, Rosedale, North Shore 0745, Auckland,
New Zealand (a division of Pearson New Zealand Ltd) • Penguin Books (South Africa) (Pty) Ltd, 24 Sturdee Avenue, Rosebank, Johannesburg 2196,
South Africa • Penguin Books Ltd, Registered Offices: 80 Strand, London WC2R 0RL, England

Text copyright © 2008 by Marjorie Blain Parker
Illustrations copyright © 2008 by Mike Wohnoutka
All rights reserved.

CIP DATA IS AVAILABLE.

Published in the United States by Dutton Children's Books,
a division of Penguin Young Readers Group
345 Hudson Street, New York, New York 10014
www.penguin.com/youngreaders

Designed by Sara Reynolds and Abby Kuperstock

Manufactured in China
ISBN 978-0-525-47950-5
Special Markets ISBN 978-0-525-42182-5 Not for Resale
1 3 5 7 9 10 8 6 4 2

This Imagination Library edition is published by Penguin Group (USA), a Pearson
company, exclusively for Dolly Parton's Imagination Library, a not-for-profit
program designed to inspire a love of reading and learning, sponsored in part by The
Dollywood Foundation. Penguin's trade editions of this work are available wherever
books are sold.

For Bill Blain, my dad,
who's always happy
when this kid comes home
M.B.P.

For my mom
M.W.

Dandelion Duckling loved his Mama Quack. And Dandelion's Mama completely loved him back. She loved him from the top of his downy head to the bottom of his webby feet, from the tip of his glossy bill to his tail of fuzzy feathers.

"Stay with me and you will be safe," Mama Quack told Dandelion.

And he always was.

But one day Dandelion wanted to explore . . . alone.
Mama Quack fretted.

"Not by yourself," she said. "There is danger in the water, danger in the air, danger on the shore, danger everywhere!"

"I'll be okay," promised Dandelion. "And I'll stay close by—just over there with Dragonfly."

So Mama Quack let him go.

"Hello, Dragonfly," said Dandelion. "I'm on an adventure. Will you race with me?"

Of course she would! Dragonfly loved dashing and darting between lily pads. Ready—set—go!

Dandelion paddled his webbed feet—*slap, slap, slap.* Dragonfly fluttered her windowpane wings— *flit, flit, flit.*

Neither noticed the pike prowling in the pond.

But Mama Quack did.

"*QUACK! QUACK! QUACK! QUACK!*" she warned them.

On the double, Dandelion scooted back and hid under Mama Quack's wing—where he stayed until the mosquitoes started buzzing.

But the next day Dandelion was eager to go discovering again.

"Remember the pike?" Mama Quack said.

"I know. I forgot to watch the water," said Dandelion. "Just let me go past the hollow log— to play with Little Polliwog."

Mama Quack sighed and let him go.

"Hello, Polliwog," said Dandelion. "I'm on an adventure. Will you blow bubbles with me?"

Of course he would! Polliwog loved gurgling and burbling in the cool pool. Ready—set—go!

Dandelion puffed fizzy air bubbles—*pop, pop, pop.* Polliwog blew billowy water bubbles—*blub, blub, blub.*

Neither noticed the hawk hunting above the horsetails.

But Mama Quack did.
"*QUACK! QUACK! QUACK! QUACK!*" she
warned them—and not a second too soon!

Dandelion zipped and zoomed, zigged and zagged,
all the way back to Mama Quack—and he didn't
budge until the frogs hushed their peeping.

But in the morning Dandelion was as curious as ever.

"Remember the hawk?" Mama Quack said.

"I'm sorry. I forgot to watch the water or the air," said Dandelion. "Give me one more chance. Just as far as the leafy reeds—to visit with the Centipedes."

Mama Quack gave him a long cuddle and let him go.

"Hello, Centipedes," said Dandelion. "I'm on an adventure. Will you have a nibbling contest with me?"

Of course they would! The Centipedes loved chomping and chewing on pond plants. Ready—set—go!

Dandelion dabbled for seeds and shoots—*crunch, crunch, crunch*. The Centipedes grazed on greens and grasses—*munch, munch, munch*.

Nobody noticed the weasel waiting in the willows.

Not even Mama Quack.

But suddenly, Dandelion stopped and looked around.

Danger!

It wasn't in the water.

It wasn't in the air.

It was . . . on the shore!

"QUACK! QUACK! QUACK! QUACK!" he warned his Mama.

The weasel pounced, its sharp teeth flashing.

But Mama was quick . . . and the weasel went splashing.

Dandelion Duckling loved his Mama Quack. And Dandelion's Mama completely loved him back. She loved him from the top of his downy head to the bottom of his webby feet, from the tip of his glossy bill to his tail of fuzzy feathers.

"Be careful and you will stay safe," Mama Quack told Dandelion.